THINGS TO KNOW HAVE AND DO AS YOU GRADUATE FROM HIGH SCHOOL

THINGS TO KNOW HAVE AND DO AS YOU GRADUATE FROM HIGH SCHOOL

ROSEMARY JENKINS

Contents

Preface   7

Introduction   9

1. Things To Know   13
2. Things To Have   19
3. Things to Do   24

Glossary   29
About the Author   33

Preface

The information I have prepared is especially dedicated to those who are preparing to graduate from high school. I am of the opinion that if I had known and done most of the things I outlined in this book while I was preparing to graduate from high school, I would have experienced a much smoother transition from girlhood to womanhood.

I have often heard people say, "You can learn from your mistakes." However, I believe that some mistakes are really not worth making. Many times, it may take too many times for a mistake to be learned from, causing people to be unproductive in their lives for too long.

I believe many mistakes can be avoided, especially if we are aware of them or know how to prepare to respond to various situations.

Introduction

As you transition from girlhood or boyhood to womanhood or manhood, it is time to accept challenges and responsibilities for your future. Setting goals is recommended in order to be productive citizens, which will enhance the quality of your life as well as others.

I recommend that you put forth a plan of action for your future goals by first determining the purpose for setting your goals and, second, determining how you will carry out your goals. It is important that you set your own goals because if you don't, someone else or something else will set your goals for you.

When someone else or something else sets goals for you, they may not have your best interest at heart. They may also set certain standards for you that you may not be able to obtain at certain times in your life.

This may cause you to turn to activities and situations that can lead to a confused and unproductive way of life.

Again, I recommend that you put forth a plan of action for attaining and accomplishing your life goals. Your goals may change as you progress in life; just make sure that your plan of action also changes in order to accomplish your goals. I recommend that you first set a short-term goal(s). You may then develop long-term goals. Set short-term goals that are attainable so that you may experience the joy and knowledge of accomplishments along the way in pursuit of accomplishing your long-term goal(s).

Developing short-term goals keeps one in the mode of "keep on trucking b-a-b-y." As you progress in life, accomplishing your goals can often lead to developing or knowing who you really are. In other words, the process you go through to accomplish your goals can help you determine your likes and dislikes, your strengths, and the areas you will need to develop.

As you graduate from high school or prepare to graduate from high school, several factors are involved in obtaining your goal(s).

This book is designed to assist you in preparing for your future as you prepare to graduate from high school. These are the things I think would make you say hum-mm-m. Some factors I will share with you may or may not apply to you. Take what you can use to develop your own plan of action.

At the end of this book, I have included a glossary for you to go to look up words that can help you better understand the terminology I am sharing with you.

Note Pages are included in the back of this book, so you may write down some factors that can help you in the future. There may be information not discussed in this book but is being discussed with you by your family, friends and significant others in your life. Note Pages in the back of this book are a good place to jot down notes.

My intention is not to take up much of your time. Please, just take a few minutes to sit back, relax, maybe snack on your favorite food and beverage and enjoy reading this book.

For it is my pleasure to share with you "Things to Know Have and Do As You Graduate From High School."

ONE

Things To Know

(HOWEVER, NOT AN ABSOLUTE)

THINGS TO KNOW ARE those things that will help you build confidence in yourself so that you may be self-sufficient. When you are confident in yourself, you are able to "hold on, baby" when life issues become a challenge for you. You will also enjoy life better.

Know that others are not responsible for making you happy.

They can enhance your life but cannot define who you are. As my ancestors would say, "When you know that you know, that you know, who you are," you have the stamina to take charge and master your life with love, joy and peace.

I recommend that you always know how to manage your money, whether it is two dollars or two hundred thousand dollars. Select your preferred banking method(s), such as using debit cards, writing checks, using credit cards, etc.

There are various banking systems you can use for your savings and spending, as well as accumulating financial stability. You may research the various resources by visiting those institutions you see advertised in the newspaper, radio, television, internet and/or recommendations from family and friends. Spending seems to be the most challenging area for many of us when it comes to managing our money. I recommend you always spend money based on the balance in your checkbook or your record-keeping method rather than the balance shown at your banking center. The money you have spent may not have cleared or gone through your banking center at the time you review your balance from them.

Remember, it is important to be able to save money for "rainy days" to come about. This is when unexpected or non-budgeted expenses occur, and you don't have the money to pay or at least assist with paying for "whatever the situation may be." Therefore, I recommend you start with a plan of action, which is called a budget. Believe me when I say a budget will let you know how much money you have, what expenses you need to pay and what money you don't have to spend. Budget planning can also help develop the creativity that you did not know you had. There are resources available to help you with budgeting, and I am not sure if I should recommend your family and friends who may not ... anyway, I will interject here: list all of your expenses and miscellaneous spending in a column, also include your money for your savings as an expense. List each month across the top of your page. Draw horizontal lines to also make columns between each month as you pay each expense.

Make a check mark beside that expense under each month to indicate that you have paid each expense that month. Determine how much you will allow for miscellaneous spending to include, but not limited to, entertainment, eating out, buying gifts, taking a trip, etc. (This should be determined after obligated expenses are paid, such as telephone bills, rent if applicable, car payments, credit card charges, utilities and etc.)

No matter how much money or material gains you will accumulate in life, learn how to manage or assist in managing it. You are to look to yourself to always have your best interest at heart.

It is important to know how to use domestic skills such as cooking, ironing, washing clothes, washing cars, doing dishes, mopping, and vacuuming the floors. No! You are not expected to become a gourmet cook; however, knowing how to cook at least breakfast foods such as eggs, toast, pancakes, grits, and other small dishes can be prepared at any time during the day;

knowing how to separate clothes by colors and/or fabrics, using appropriate cleaning agents can help you maintain yourself. Know how to master or perform these domestic skills at a level that is comfortable for you to perform in a time of need. There may be times when the weather may not permit you to travel, broken relationships may occur, and low finances may cause you to need to cut back on your spending, which can be examples of a time in need. A time of need may also occur when others are not around you or available to perform these skills for you to survive. Rather than becoming helpless or frustrated, you will know how to perform these skills yourself. Knowing how to perform these skills at your comfort level can make life a whole lot more rewarding for you as you will look to yourself and not have to depend on others always.

For those of you who will decide to go to work right after high school (and for those of you who will pursue advanced education or training, this will come for you later), make sure that you know how to look for work to include, but not limited to completing job applications, preparing a resume with cover letters, interviewing skills, appropriate dress and questions to ask the interviewer, networking and etc. Various resources are available for assistance, such as school guidance counselors, newspapers, the Internet, government agencies, family and friends.

If you have a health problem, make sure that you will know how to maintain your health in the future. Your parents or guardian may not be available all the time in the future to tell you when to take your medications or treatments. It is important that you know how your health problem will affect your future; therefore, you are better able to determine your lifestyle as you continue with your health maintenance. Speak with your healthcare provider(s), parents or guardian, and research the library, internet, contact health organizations, attend workshops and utilize other forms of assistance.

For those of you who do not have a health problem, you can maintain your health with at least an annual medical examination using the resources above for assistance. Other health issues or concerns involve knowing or perhaps continuing your practice of abstinence from sex, using protection during sex, birth control, venereal diseases and the effects of alcohol and drug abuse. (As we age, these things affect our bodies differently, even in the little time from being a junior in high school to being a sophomore in college).

Before an emergency occurs, such as a fire, a friend or family member passing out, or an automobile breakdown, always have a plan of action.

Think of possible emergency situations and plan how you will respond. Remember, when in doubt in almost any given area, there is usually "911."

TWO

Things To Have

(HOWEVER, NOT AN ABSOLUTE)

THINGS TO HAVE ARE those things that help us to get along with ourselves and maintain order with others.

Have someone you can talk to on a consistent basis to express your joys, sorrows, opinions, likes, dislikes, etc. I find that this helps to keep peace within me. You may talk to a family counselor, pastor, family member, friend, significant other, etc. Just make sure that you are comfortable talking to them. This is also a time when you may find out what "trust" is really all about. Have a place where you can go to interact with those who can help you to develop as a loving, joyous, and peaceful person. Many people interact with various organizations, churches, and synagogues or develop something on their own. It is important that the place(s) you interact with help you maintain a peaceful and healthy spirit.

Have a sense of spirituality. Many of us find comfort in believing in a higher being. For me, it is God. Consult with your parents or guardian, friends, and church leaders, and visit various spiritual places that may aid you in determining how you can develop your spirituality.

Have a sense of humor. Be able to laugh at yourself with yourself and others. Many things and situations we can change in life. Many we may not be able to do so at that moment or not at all; it may be good to find the humor in the situation and move on to something else. And if deemed necessary, come back to that situation at a later date for those of you who don't give up easily.

Have fun, whether it is partying at a friend's house or a nightclub, playing games, making funny faces, or going on an advantageous outing. Just be sure to show respect for others as they are also having fun.

Have a means of transportation. This include, but are not limited to being transported by your girlfriend or boyfriend in their automobile, public transportation service, taxi, bicycle, or other authorized automobiles on the road. When you buy or lease an automobile, down payments are often required, and financing is needed if you do not have enough money to pay for the automobile in one lump sum. Depending on who or where you buy or lease your automobile determines the type of financing that will be available to you. Since financing often involves determining if you are credit-worthy at your age, co-signers are usually required to lease or buy your automobile. Automobiles are available to lease or purchase through various means, such as individuals, agencies, banks, and automobile dealerships. At some point in your life, you have to experience working with a car salesperson (though not an absolute).

When you buy or lease an automobile, you have insurance to cover liability and, if required, collision damages (both are usually required if you have not paid for the automobile in full). Consult with your parents or guardian as well as an insurance agent to explain what is required to obtain these insurances. If you drive without the required insurance, legal problems for you, as well as others involved, may become "out of control."

Other insurances to have are health, life and insurance for your things or property, including rental insurance. This applies to those of you who will be living on your own as well as those of you who will be going off to a school of higher education. Consult your parents or guardian as well as an insurance agent to explain further.

Have a place to live. Some of you will go away to college and stay in a dormitory. Others will stay at home or rent an apartment or house. Some of you may even be able to buy a house. Consider these factors: for dormitories, make sure you make an application at your school of choice prior to the deadline. If possible, make arrangements with the housing director at your school of choice to visit the dormitory to access space, layout, etc. You will then know what is appropriate for you to take with you when you move in (this will help with some of the space issues roommates often encounter at school). Consider if you can or will select your roommate (private dormitory rooms are sometimes available if you do not want a roommate).

Renting a house or an apartment usually involves filling out applications and completing the necessary paperwork. The landlord or property manager may request a non-refundable application fee and conduct a credit check (at this point in your life, some landlords or property managers may request for you to have a co-signer). If you are accepted as a renter, you may also be requested to pay a deposit upfront and pay the first month's rent. The deposit is usually equal to or less than the rent amount. You may ask all potential landlords and property managers about all applicable fees and rules prior to your pursuit of renting from them. You may be asked to sign a lease. Point of Note: Each local governing area has rules in place that state your rights as a tenant, whether you signed a lease or not.

Buying a house or common sharing dwelling usually involves several factors. This is especially so since there are various means of financing a house these days. However, some familiar factors include locating a house on your own or perhaps working with a real estate agent. You may be asked to make a down payment or some form of deposit, which may be referred to as earnest money, prior to approval for financing. You will go through the qualifying process in order to be approved for financing to buy a house. You may have to provide the bank or lending institution documentation of various information about yourself, such as your income, place of employment, money available, creditors, credit history, etc. (Again, co-signers may be required at your age.) You may consult with a real estate agent, bank or lending institution, family and friends who have purchased a home(s) for more details or involvement with this process.

Note: When you have to make payments on your financing amount, interest is usually charged or added to your payments. Interest rates vary. Consult the resources mentioned above for assistance.

THREE

Things to Do

(HOWEVER, NOT AN ABSOLUTE)

THINGS TO DO ARE those things that you take action on that will aid you in accomplishing your goals. You will also do this with everything else in life.

Open a banking account, which may consist of a checking and/or savings account. You may check with various banking centers to see who may offer services that are most suitable for you at this time. Have your parents or guardian assist you in opening a checking and or savings account. Also, note that they may require that you have employment to be able to open and maintain your own checking and or savings account.

Do establish a line of credit. This is a good time for you to begin to establish that you are credit-worthy. Throughout the rest of your life, many things you will try to accomplish socially and financially will tie into your credit, which may affect you when getting a job.

Pay your bills on time. Some of you already have credit cards, and for those of you who do not, this may be a good way for you to start establishing your credit-worthiness. You may also consult the resources noted above for assistance.

Do know how to read and use your local newspapers. Newspapers often contain just about any information in life that you may require or desire, such as sports, entertainment, employment, grocery shopping, advertisement, clothing, and other personal and household items for sale, stock market reviews, housing, etc.

Treat people as you want them to treat you.

Greet others with a smile, handshake, hug, high five, or other pleasant mannerisms when appropriate.

Do your best to try to get along with others. When possible, avoid gossip, back-biting, jealousy, envy and other behaviors that add to negative behaviors within us. We then often express the results of our negative behaviors toward others. Remember that a kind relationship makes a healthy relationship.

When others give me something, I often say "thank you," and I recommend you do the same. This is just called common courtesy, which I do not see much of these days. Remember, when you give something to someone, such as a gift, don't always expect a gift or some other favor in return. When you give to others, do it with the mindset of feeling good for having been able to do so.

Do register to vote. Voting is essential in our lives, and our lifestyle will be greatly affected by many of the decisions that are determined through your voting.

Do maintain good hygiene. Parents or guardians may not be around as they were in elementary, junior high and high school, telling you to take a bath, brush your teeth, comb your hair, wash your clothes, put on some deodorant, etc. If you do not maintain good hygiene, don't be surprised when others avoid you as much as they can.

Do carry with you at all times a form of identification that may include your driver's license or other picture identification. Consult your school, family and friends, government agencies, your local telephone directory etc., on how you can obtain a form of identification. You may also consult with your resources as to the most acceptable form of identification used in your area.

Do consider learning or being trained for more than one skill or trade due to today's ever-changing technology. When changes occur that may affect your area of skill or trade; you can continue to have the means to maintain your self-sufficiency by doing the other skill or trade.

Do show respect for our senior citizens at all times. This is just a good humanitarian thing to do. When possible, it is good to listen to their rich history; absolutely no profane language is spoken in their presence. Do some things they may ask of you that will cause "no sweat off your back," open the door when they are near you, speak to them with a smile or perhaps sit down with them for a cup of coffee... Okay, so you don't drink coffee... Would it be more appealing if I said: How about a latte?

Glossary

Boyhood -- Period of time for boys or males under 18 years old.

Budget -- A written plan or outline of your expenses.

Co-Signer -- Someone who, along with you, will be held responsible for the payments to be made on what you are using or borrowing. The co-signer is usually someone who is credit-worthy.

Credit History -- Your past record showing the frequency of how you paid back what you used or borrowed. In other words, did you pay on time, late or no time.

Credit Worthy -- You are worth taking a risk on to loan money or other goods. (Your credit history will play a big role in this decision)

Creditors -- Those who you owe for the things you bought or leased.

Earnest Money -- Money you put down to confirm that you are serious or earnest about wanting to lease or buy an item.

Financing -- From the balance of what you owe, a lending institution will pay in full to whomever you are buying or leasing an item from. You will, in turn, pay the lending institution in installments with interest.

Girlhood -- Period of time for girls or females under 18 years old.

Goals -- What you want to accomplish or gain.

Interest -- A rate of charge or money added to your financed amount after having a lending institution loan you money.

Landlord/Property Manager -- One or more persons responsible for managing all of the business associated with a property, such as a house, an apartment, townhomes and other lodging units. Payments for rent are usually paid to the Landlord or Property Manager. They enforce the terms of a lease or rental agreement.

Lease -- A written agreement between you and a Landlord or Property Manager outlining the terms of the lease. (Some may say the rental agreement). The lease terms may include, but are not limited to, specifying the start date of the lease, who will be responsible for paying rent, the termination date, deposits required, other fees, rental rules, policies, etc.

Lending Institution -- Banks and other businesses

that have money to loan you so you can purchase or lease your good (s).

Line of Credit -- A build-up of creditors whom you have or are making payments to suggest that you are credit-worthy. Should you prove to be credit-worthy, some lending institutions will allow you to spend a set amount of money when it is convenient for you without you having to continue to go through the financing process each time you want to borrow money.

Manhood -- A period of time for men or males over 18 years old.

Means -- A way of.

Rainy Days -- Unexpected situations occur.

Respect -- Displaying or acknowledging that you care about something or someone. Having high regard for something or someone.

(S) -- Makes the word plural. More than one.

Spirituality -- Your inner awareness that drives you to clarify what is right or wrong as well as your likes or dislikes.

Womanhood -- A Period of time for women or females over 18 years old.

YA -- Young Adult(s).

About the Author

Rosemary Jenkins is a native of Shreveport, Louisiana. She resides in North Central Texas. Jenkins earned a Bachelor of Science in Speech and Theatre Education and a Master of Education in Counseling and School Psychology. She is also a Certified Rehabilitation Counselor. While having reflected on her own life adventures, Jenkins states that too often, many of our life mistakes can take us too long to recover when we have not equipped ourselves to manage them better. Jenkins also stated that a crucial time to prepare for such is during high school as we are preparing to graduate.